Cooking For Life Begins With You

Recipes For Life!

Dorothy Massey

authorHOUSE®

AuthorHouse™
1663 Liberty Drive
Bloomington, IN 47403
www.authorhouse.com
Phone: 1-800-839-8640

First published by AuthorHouse 7/7/2009

ISBN: 978-1-4490-0543-6 (sc)

Printed in the United States of America
Bloomington, Indiana

This book is printed on acid-free paper.

BREAKFAST

Asparagus Omelet

spray olive oil

1 teaspoon sea salt

3 asparagus spears

1 teaspoon of pepper

2 eggs

Directions:

In skillet, lightly spray olive oil on medium heat. Cut asparagus in half and place in skillet. Beat 2 eggs in mixing bowl, spread eggs over asparagus.

Add salt and pepper. Fold omelet over, add swiss chesse on top. Compliment with fresh fruit and slice of toast.

Moma Cinnamon Raisins Toast

2 slice raisins bread

1 teaspoon ground cinnamon

1 tablespoon butter

1 tablespoon sugar

Directions:

Spread butter on bread. Sprinkle sugar and cinnamon on bread.

Toast in a toaster oven for 3 minutes until golden brown.

Yummy Potatoes & Bacon

4 large potates

1 whole green bell pepper (chopped big)

1 whole red bell pepper (chopped big)

1 whole sweet onion (chopped)

1 teaspoon sea salt

1 teaspoon black pepper

1/8 cup oil

1 pound of bacon

Directions:

In skillet, fry bacon until lightly brown. Drain grease on absorbent paper. Set aside.

In skillet, add oil. Wash and peel potatoes, cut ¾ inch thick. Place in skillet, cook over meduim heat until brown on one side, add bell peppers, and onion to potateos. Cover with lid tightly. Simmer 20 minutes until tender. Cut bacon in half slices, add to potatoes Now add salt and black pepper.

Dorothy's Tip : On 1 pound sliced bacon, spinkle 1/8 cup of sugar for crispiness.

Dot Sunrise Spinach Omelet

2 eggs beat well or organic eggs

1/8 teaspoon white pepper

3 tablespoons milk or natural soy milk

4 fresh spinach leaves

1/8 teaspoon chopped green onion

Spray olives oil

1 slice Lorraine Swiss cheese

Directions:

 In small mixing bowl, add eggs and beat well. Combine milk, and pepper in well.

Spray olive oil in skillet; add onions cook on medium heat for 3 minutes. Now add beaten eggs cook for 5 minutes.

Add spinach fold in half add cheese. You can garnish with chives for extra flavor.

Canadain Bacon Style

1 pound Canadian bacon sliced

3 eggs beaten well

1/4 cup green bell pepper chopped

1/4 cup white onion chopped

(1) 12 ounce package shredded hash brown potatoes (store bought)

1/8 teaspoon pepper

1/8 teaspoon salt

1 cup shredded cheddar cheese

2 tablespoons olives oil

Directions:

In skillet on medium heat, pour in oil add potatoes cook for 15 minutes cover with lid.

Reduce heat to low add bacon cook for 10 minutes.

In a mixing bowl, beat eggs. Combine bell pepper, onion, salt, and pepper.

Pour egg mixer over potatoes, and bacon, cook for 5 minutes stir well.

Sprinkle cheese, turn heat off, cover with lid until ready to serve.

Dorothy's Tip: *When frying meat, try sprinkling paprika over it, so it will turn golden brown.*

Sausage & Gravy

½ pound ground turkey sausage or pork sausage

1 cup milk

2 tablespoons corn starch

1/8 teaspoon sea salt

1/8 teaspoon black pepper

Directions:

In skillet on medium heat, brown sausage for 6 minutes. Drain grease.

In a small mixing cup add milk, corn starch, salt, and pepper. Stir until completely dissolved.

Add mixer to sausage, reduce to low heat and cook for 5 minutes.

Serve on top biscuits.

Oats for breakfast with Fresh Fruit

May add cream and butter (optional)

1 cup steel cut oats or old fashioned oats

1 ½ cups water

½ cup strawberry slice

¼ cup blueberries

¼ cup raspberries

¼ cup blackberries

Directions:

In a pot, bring water to a boil. Slowly stir in the steel cut oats, cook for 5 minutes or until oats begin to thicken.

Reduce heat, simmer for about 20 minutes. You can serve with milk and cream or patch of butter. Great with fresh fruit!

Dorothy's twist: serve with nuts and pinch of cinnamon.

Tip: Want to enjoy your chicken salad? Then add fresh fruits like blueberries and strawberries.

Tip: Try rolling lunchmeat, cheese, banana pepper, bean sprout with no bread for light lunch.

Ham & Gravy

1 pound lean ham steak

¼ cup sweet onion

½ cup water

Directions:

In skillet on medium heat, cook ham and onion. Cover with lid tightly for 10 minutes until brown on one side.

Remove lid brown on other side. Reduce heat to low and slowly add in water, simmer for 10 minutes. Serve with biscuit and potatoes. Enjoy!

Helpful hints on Steak

Marinate over night for juicy, tender steak and ready for grill or oven, uhm so good.

½ cup steak sauce

¼ cup Worcestershire

2 teaspoons soy sauce

2 tablespoons pineapple juice

Add all ingredients together and rub on both sides on for juicy & tender steak.

LUNCH

Hot Turkey Sandwiches

4 slices smoked turkey breast

1 ounce aged sharp cheese

1 ounce baby swiss cheese

2 slices bread (your preference)

3 spinach leaves

1 teaspoon butter

Directions:

In a skilliet over medium heat, spread butter on one slide of each piece of bread. Then place the bread in the skillet.

Add aged sharp cheese on one piece of bread and baby swiss on the other. Place turkey and spinach on top of cheese. Brown both sides of sandwich in skillet until golden brown. Slice in half.

Make this recipe your own by serving with fresh fruit such as strawberries, oranges, or grapes. This is a great treat for kids!

Crescent Turkey Bacon Sandwiches

6 slices turkey bacon

2 tablespoon mayonnaise

2 slices tomatoes

6 spinah leaves

2 Crescent Rolls

Directions:

In skillet, fry bacon on each side until brown. Drain absorbent paper.

Slice crescent in half add mayonnaise, spainch leaves, tomatos and bacon.

Enjoy lunch with fresh fruit. Makes 2 servings.

Garden Sub Sandwich

6 slices turkey or favorite lunchmeat

1 French sub bread

3 slices of baby swiss cheese

4 sweet cherry peppers

3 banana peppers

3 olives green and black

4 slices of cucumber

3 slices of tomtoes

2 tablespoon mayonnaise

3 slices of onion

6 spanich leaves

¾ cup of lettuce

Directions:

Slice bread in half. Add mayonnaise, lettuce, onion, peppers, tomatos, lunchment and cheese. Then add olives and cucumber. Enjoy! Makes 2 servings.

This recipe is great with your favorite potato chips!

Yield to the word of God to give way to physical force and flexible submissive. This book is from God.

Coney Dog

1 pound beef hot dogs

1 pound ground turkey (85/15%) lean or ground beef (85/15%) lean

3 tablespoons chill powder

2 tablespoons ground cumin

¼ cup chill bean

½ cup water

¼ cup sweet pickle

½ cup shredded cheese

(1) 6 ounce can tomato paste

Directions:

In skillet, brown turkey on medium heat for 10 minutes, drain. Add chill powder, and cumin, stir well cook for 5 minutes.

Add water, stir in pickle, paste, and stir well. Reduce to low heat add chill bean and simmer for 10 minutes.

In another skillet, boil ¼ cup of water and boil hot dog for 5 minutes.

Serve on hot dog bun, add cheese on top. So Good!!

Fish Taco

~~~~~~

1 pound strips of cod or halibut fish

4 taco shells

½ cup lettuce chopped

1 package fish taco seasoning

1 plastic bag

2 tablespoons oil

Directions:

Place ½ strips of fish, oil, fish taco seasoning in bag, and shake well for marinating. In skillet, on medium heat place fish strips in skillet cook fish for 8 to 10 minutes.

Add fish inside shells, top with lettuce.

Deep Fried Fish

2 pounds whole fish, fillets

1 teaspoon sea salt

1-2 teaspoon fish seasoning

1 cup cornmeal or fine dried bread crumbs

3 cups cooking oil deep

Season fish on both sides with salt and fish seasons.

Directions:

Pour oil in skillet on high heat allow oil to warm. Dip fish into cornmeal and place in oil.

Brown on oneside, turn down to medium heat then brown the other side. Once fish is done enjoy with fish dip. Makes 4 servings.

Dorothy's Twist: *Spink fish seasonings and lemon pepper on both sides of fish for great favor.*

Home Style Pull Pork On Bun

2 pounds Boston butt or substitute with Turkey Thighs

3 tablespoon hickory smoked flavor

2 tablespoon season salt

1 ½ cup water

Directions:

Rub hickory smoked on meat well. Add season salt.

Place in slow cooker (crock pot). Add water, and cook on high heat for 3 hours until fork tender. Drain off juice and remove bones from meat.

Add your flavor BBQ Sauce. Enjoy this great tasting food.

Makes 8 servings.

Tip: For better flavor, marinate meat over night and place in refrigerator.

Pork burger Patties

1 pound ground pork

¼ cup red bell pepper chopped

¼ cup yellow bell pepper chopped

¼ cup sweet onion chopped

1 teaspoon sea salt

spray olive oil

Directions:

In large bowl, combine all ingredients well together, form patties.

In skillet, on medium heat add oil. Fry patties on one side for 8 minutes, turn over.

Reduce heat on low. Cover tightly with lid, simmer and let brown for 5 minutes on other side. Serve on bun. Ohm Good!

Vegetable Pizza

12 inch pizza crust (store bought)

1 white onion peel and dice

1 sweet onion peel and dice

1 medium red bell pepper dice

1 medium yellow bell pepper dice

1 medium orange bell pepper dice

8 ounce pizza sauce

1 ½ cup mozzarella cheese

Spray olive oil

Directions:

Roll crust out and place on pizza pan. Add sauce to crust, spread evenly, and set aside. Wash all vegetables. In skillet, add all vegetables and spray well with oil.

Cook for 10 minutes on medium heat. Drain juice from the skillet; add cooked vegetables to the crust.

Top with cheese and bake 350 f for 15 to 20 minutes until edges are brown. Yummy Pizza you'll enjoy. Makes 6 servings.

Dorothy's Tip: *A dull knife cuts cheese better than a sharp knife. A warm knife cuts cheese like butter.*

DINNER

Cream Alfredo Broccoli Pasta

1 package of alfredo sauce

1/8 teaspoon sea salt

½ cup grated parmesan cheese

1 ½ teaspoon melts butter

2 cups broccoli

8 ounces package of pasta (store bought)

1 ½ cup milk

2 ½ cups water

Directions:

In a pot, combine milk, butter, and package of alredo sauce over medium heat until contents are dissolved. Add salt, cheese and stir constently for 20 minutes. Remove from heat. Set aside.

In another pot, boil water for 5 minutes. Add pasta until tender. Drain pasta.

In another pot, steam broccoli for 3 minutes.

Pour Alfredo sauce, and steam broccoli over cooked pasta. Enjoy

Makes 4 servings

Dorothy's Twist; *To prepare the perfect tasty chicken: Soak chicken in 3 cups of cold water and 3 tablespoon of Sea Salt. Place in refrigerator overnight. The following day, rinse chicken well in cold water. Then add your favorite chicken seasoning or lemon pepper.*

Italian Sausage
skillet or grill

1 pound smoked sausage links

1 green bell pepper chopped

1 red bell pepper chopped

1 orange bell pepper chopped

1 sweet onion chopped

1 white onion chopped

Directions:

In a skillet over medium heat, cut sausage and place in skillet. Add peppers and onions, cook until meat is brown. Turn over meat only once. Cover tightly with lid. Simmer 20 minutes.

Makes 6 servings.

Sloppy Dot

1 pound ground turkey

¼ cup chopped onion

1 cup water

6 ounce can of tomato paste

1 package of sloppy Joe seasoning

1 teaspoon of Cumin

¼ cup of relish

Directions:

In skillet, cook meat and onion on medium heat for 10 minutes. Drain well.

Add sloppy Joe seasoning, cumin, relish and water into skillet. Slowly add tomato paste.

Stir in well, and simmer for 10 minutes. Add to bread or bun.

Turkey Meat Loaf

1 pound ground turkey

½ pound ground turkey sausage

1 package of dry onion soup

1 ½ cup bread crumbs

2 eggs

1/8 cup cerely chopped

1 ½ cup ketchup

1/8 cup green bell pepper chopped

½ teaspoon sea salt

Directions:

Combine all ingredients in a large mixing bowl. Mix well firm meat into a loaf and bake at 350oF for 30 minutes. Add ketchup on top (optional). Yummy!

Beef Meat Loaf

1 pound ground beef

½ pound ground sirloin

½ pound sausage

1 ½ teaspoon sea salt

1/8 cup bell pepper chopped

2 eggs

1 cup bread crumbs

1 package dry onion soup

1 ½ cup ketchup

1/8 cup celery

Directions:

Combine all ingredients in a large mixing bowl. Mix well, firm mean into a loaf and bake at 350 oF for 45 to 50 minutes. Add ketchup on top (optional).

Dorothy's Twist: *Wash and peel 1 large baken potato, place potato inside meat loaf. So that when you slice you get meat and potatos. Add veggies for a great dinner.*

Lasagna

1 pound hamburger or ground turkey

2 cups mozzarella cheese

1 pound cottage cheese

½ box lasagna noodles, cooked

16 ounce pasta sauce

1 egg

1 teaspoon of parsley flakes

1 ½ oregano leaves

12 ounces of whole tomato, drain juice

½ cup ricotta cheese

3 tablespoon grated parmesain cheese

Directions:

In skillet over medium heat, brown meat and drain. Add sauce and tomato to cooked meat.

In large bowl, mix egg, cottage cheese, ricotta cheese, oregano, parsley, salt and pepper.

Layer noodles, meat sauce, cottage cheese mixture, and mozzarella cheese. Repeat and bake for 55 minutes at 375oF.

Add parmesain cheese on top, when ready to serve.

Beef Stew

1 pound Stew meat or short ribs, cut up

1 package dried onion soup mix

(1) 10 ounce can cream of mushroom soup

(1) 10 ounce can of cream of celery soup

1 ½ cup water

1 can whole corn

2 tablespoon olive oil

Add in desired amount of:

Carrots peeled and chopped

Potatoes peeled and chopped

Onions peeled and chopped

Clerley chopped

Directions:

In skillet, on medium heat brown meat with oil and half package of dried onion soup for 8 minutes on each side.

Place meat, onion soup and water in crock pot, cook for 1:45 minutes, make sure meat is tender.

Combine all other ingredients cook in crock pot for a remain 1 hour on high temperature. Cook on low temperature for another 30 minutes.

Dorothy's Twist: *When cooking with short ribs the stew has more flavor because of the bone. So you can cook with half stew meat and half short ribs for great flavor and vareity of meats.*

Tuna Casserole

10 ounce can condensed cream of chicken soup

¼ cup milk

6 small red potatoes (washed & sliced)

1/8 cup celery

½ cup peas & carrots (frozen store bought)

¼ cup shredded cheddar cheese

1 can of tuna

Directions:

Combine soup and milk in a 2 –quart casserole dish. Add tuna, red patato, peas & carrots and celery. Sprinkle cheese on top.

Cover with alumunial foil and bake at 350oF for 30 to 35 minutes until cheese begins to bubble.

Crab cakes patties

1 pound crab meat

¼ cup bread crumbs

2 tablespoons mayonnaise

2 teaspoon seafood seasoning

2 teaspoon parsley flakes

1 teaspoon Dijon mustard

1 egg beaten

1/8 teaspoon sea salt

Directions:

In medium bowl, add mayonnaise, fish season, parsley, mustard, and egg.

Stir in crab meat, salt and bread crumbs. Shape mixture into patties bake in oven at 325oF for 10 minutes or fry on medium heat with olive oil until golden brown on each side.

Salmon patties

1 cans 16 ounce salmon (boneless)

1 cup bread crumbs

1 egg

¼ cup white onion

¼ cup green bell pepper

1/8 teaspoon sea salt

½ cup oil

Directions:

In a large bowl, combine egg, bread, onion, pepper, and salt, mix well.

In skillet, on medium heat, pour oil. Form patties and fry on both sides for 5 minutes. Drain on absorbent paper. Enjoy with a bowl of rice!

Liver Wrap in Bacon

1 pound bacon

1 pound beef liver or calf liver

1 teaspoon sea salt

1 teaspoon black pepper

1 small white onion diced in small piece

1 small green bell pepper diced small piece

¼ cup unbleached flour- whole wheat

1/3 cup oil

Directions:

In plastic bag, combine salt, pepper, flour and liver shake until covered. Pour oil in skillet, place liver in skillet on medium heat. Before placing liver in skillet make sure oil is hot.

Add pepper and onion on medium heat cook until liver is brown on each side 10 to 15 minutes. Drain on absorbent paper, set a side.

In skillet on medium heat, fry bacon on both sides 15 minutes until brown. Drain on absorbent paper. Allow bacon to cool down for 5 minutes.

Wrap bacon over liver and place a toothpick in center to hold in place. Place liver wrap on cookie sheet and bake for 10 minutes at 350oF. Serve hot or cold, great for appetizers. Enjoy!

Dorothy's Tip: *When frying bacon, sprinkle small acount of salt in the pan,it keeps grease from splattering.*

Ground Turkey Taco

1 pound of ground turkey   85/15%

½ cup of water

1 package taco seasoning

1 tomato chopped

1 cup lettuce shredded

½ cup shredded cheese

½ cup chopped onion

¾ cup salsa

6 taco shells

Directions:

In skillet, cook ground turkey on medium heat for 12 minutes. Drain well.

Add seasoning and water to meat, stir until completely dissolved while still cooking on medium heat.

Once seasonings dissolved, add salsa reduce heat to low and simmer until thick. Add meat into shell and layer with lettuce, onion, tomato and cheese.

Optional add sour cream and ranch dressing.

Barbecued Spareribs/Baby Backribs

2 whole slabs of ribs

Season salt/salt pepper

Hickory smoked flavor

Aluminum Foil

Directions:

Lightly sprinkle meat with season on each side. Add 1 cap of smoked flavor on each side of meat rub in well.

Warp in foil tightly and seal, place on grill with medium heat for 1 hours 55 minutes until fork tender.

Unwrap foil; reduce heat to low and brush on your favor BBQ Sauce. Simmer for 30 minutes.

BREAD, SALAD, SIDES

Moma's Cornbread

3 tablespoon oil

2 cups self- rising meal

1 - 2 tablespoon sugar

2 eggs

Spray oil

1 ½ cup butter milk

Directions:

Combine all ingrediants in a large mixing bowl mix well. In, 0 inch pan spray oil well on all sides and bottom. Pour mixer in pan bake 25 to 30 minutes at 350oF.

Jalpeno Hot Water Cornbread

2 cups water —boil hot

2 ½ cups self rising yellow corn meal

¼ cup sugar

¼ cup flour

1 ½ teaspoon sea salt

½ cup jalapeno pepper

2½ cups oil

Directions:

Mix all dry ingredients together add boiling hot water. Mix well until thick. Place peppers into batter.

Make ¾ inch dip batter, rinse hands in cold water, round batter in plam in your hand.

Pour oil in large skillet over medium heat, then fry cornbread on both sides until golden brown about 5 minutes on each side. Drain on absorbent paper.

Makes 12 servings

Strawberry Salad

4 cups of romaine lettuce

1/8 Dry chirves

1 chopped red onion

1 whole cucumber sliced

1 pint fresh strawberries sliced

¼ cup of pecans

¼ grated parmasan cheese

Directions:

In large salad bowl, toss lettucse, onion, cucumber, and fresh strawberries.

Add your favorite dressing to coat salad. Top with pecans and parmasan cheese.

Carrot Cranberries Salad

2 cups grated carrot

½ cup dried cranberries

1/3 cup mayonnaise

1/8 cup almonds

Directions:

Combine carrots, cranberries and mayonnaise. Sprinkle almonds on top. Cover with lid, let chill until serving time.

Grandma's Good O' Potato Salad

4 large potatos

1 whole white onion

3 starks of cerely

1/3 cup sugar

1 teaspoon of sea salt

¾ cup mayonnaise

3 tablespoon sweet pickles

1/3 cup dill pickles

¼ cup of butter pickles

2 hard- boiled eggs

3 cups of boiling hot water

Directions:

In a pot, pour water and bring to a boil. Combine potatos, onion, celery, and egg for 20 minutes cover with lid.

In a large bowl, add all other ingredients together well (sugar, salt, mayonnaise, sweet pickes, dill pickles, and butter pickeles. Peel skin off potatos and dise.
Only use potato, throw away onion & celery.

Then add potatos in bowl with other ingredients, mix well. Peel hard boil eggs, slice eggs and place on top. Chill for an hour and serve. Great with any meal!

Oven or grill bake bean

(2)12ounce pork bean

1 ½ cup brown sugar

1 stalk celery

1teaspoon ground cinnamon

2 cups ketchup

2 slice pork bacon, ham, or turkey bacon

Directions:

In large pot for grilling, mix all ingredients together. Place bacon on top.

Grill for 35 minutes or bake for 1 hour. Serve hot or cold.

Grill Vegetable

1 stalk broccoli cut into pieces

6 whole asparagus

1 medium size sweet potatoes cut into pieces

1 medium size squash cut into pieces

1 medium size zucchini cut into pieces

3 whole carrots

6 green onions

Spray olive oil

Directions:

Wash and slice all vegetable in large pieces. Place vegetables on foil, spray well. Add salt and pepper, roast on grill for 15 minutes wrap tight. Unwrap foil and cook for another 15 minutes until tender.   Serve warm.

Fresh Green Bean

1 pound fresh green beans leave whole, snap off end of green beans

Or (1) 16ounce can of green beans

½ pound smoked turkey/or pork ham hock

1 whole medium white onion sliced

1 whole medium red onion sliced

2 cups water

2 teaspoons sea salt

1/8 teaspoon black pepper

1 teaspoon lemon pepper

2 tablespoons butter

Directions:

In boiling pan, combine water, smoked turkey, and onion, boil for 10 minutes on medium heat cover with lid.

Add salt, pepper, green beans, and butter, reduce heat cook on low for 30 minutes until ready to serve.

Scalloped Potatoes

4 cups thick- sliced raw baking potatoes/ peeled and rinse in cold water

1 ½ teaspoons sea salt

1/8 teaspoon black or white ground pepper

2 cups milk

2 tablespoons corn starch

1 ½ cup shredded cheese

Directions:

In casserole dish place, combine potatoes, salt, and pepper, set a side.

In small mixing bowl, mix milk and corn starch until dissolved. Pour over potatoes.

Sprinkle on cheese bake at 350o F for 35 minutes with lid. Remove lid and brown for an additional 10 minutes. Great for leftover, Enjoy!

Mashed Potatoes

4 large raw baking potatoes washed & peeled

1 ½ teaspoons sea salt

1/8 teaspoon white ground pepper

½ cup butter

¼ cup milk

¾ cup evaporated cream

Directions:

In pot, boil potatoes for 20 minutes with lid over medium heat.

Remove potatoes and place in mixing bowl. Blend on high for 5 minutes until their light and fluffy.

Add butter, milk, cream, salt and pepper. Blend on high another 5 minutes. Keep warm until serving. Smooth and Rich, Enjoy!

Fried Cabbage

1 large head cabbage cut in large piece

½ stick butter

1/ 8 teaspoon sea salt

1/8 teaspoon black pepper

1/8 teaspoon lemon pepper

Directions:

In a skillet on medium heat, add butter, cabbage, salt, and pepper for 8 minutes.

Reduce heat cook on low for 15 minutes with lid.

Dorothy's Twist: *Adding 1 cup of red cabbage for delightful color.*

Asparagus with Mango

18 spears asparagus

1 medium size mango

¼ cup butter or spray oil

1/8 teaspoon salt

1/8 teaspoon pepper

Directions:

In skillet, on medium heat melt butter, add washed asparagus. Add peeled and slice mango.

Cook for 10 minutes until tender. Add salt and pepper.

Dorothy's Twist: *This recipe can be stored in refrigerator for two or three days. You can even freeze and serve later.*

Tuna Salad

1 hard-cooked egg chopped

¼ cup mayonnaise

1/8 teaspoon salt

1/8 teaspoon pepper

1/8 teaspoon paprika

(1) 5 ounce canned tuna

¼ cup chopped onion, or celery

3 tablespoons sweet pickle

Directions:

Blend mayonnaise, salt, pepper, paprika, onion, or celery, and pickles, mix well.

Add tuna and egg. Cover with lid, let chill until serving time. You may serve on bread, bun, rolls, crackers, or tomatoes. Enjoy!

Olives Salad

1/3 cup black olives

1/3 cup green olives

¼ cup sweet piquant pepper

¼ cup Greek feta cheese

½ cup apple vinegar

3 tablespoon honey or brown sugar

¼ cup olive oil

Directions:

In medium bowl, combine all olives, oil, piquant pepper and feta cheese together.

In small mixing cup, combine vinegar and brown sugar, stir together and pour over the olives mixture. Cover with lid and chill until ready to serve.

Three bell pepper pasta Salad

1 yellow bell pepper /sliced in large piece

1 red bell pepper /sliced in large piece

1 orange bell pepper /sliced in large piece

1 sweet onion /sliced in large piece

1 red onion /sliced in large piece

½ stick butter

1 pound pasta shell

1 ½ cup Caesar dressing

½ cup parmesan cheese

Directions:

In skillet, melt butter on low heat, add pepper and onion simmer for 10 minutes, and set a side.

Boil three cup water in pot, add pasta cook for 10 minutes. Drain well, add cooked peppers to pasta.

Add dressing and parmesan cheese, chill until serving time.

Dorothy's Twist: *For the best tasty chicken salad, add fresh blueberries and strawberries.*

Scallops Salad

1 quart romaine lettuce

2 cups fresh spinach leaves

1 pound fresh scallops

3 tablespoons butter

1 teaspoon fish seasoning

1 tablespoon parmesan cheese

Directions:

In skillet, melt butter over medium heat. Add scallops and fish seasoning, cook in medium heat until scallops are brown, tender and pulling apart, set a side.

In medium bowl, add lettuce, spinach and scallops. Toss together, top with cheese and your favorite dressing.

Fried Corn

1 can cream corn

6 ear fresh corn cob/wash cut corn off cob

2 tablespoons sweet onion chopped

¼ cup green bell pepper chopped

1 teaspoon dry mustard

1/8 teaspoon salt

1/8 teaspoon black pepper

3 tablespoons butter

Directions:

In skillet, melt butter add all ingredients on medium heat for 15 minutes until thick.

Reduce heat to low for 5 minutes. Serve as a side dish.

DESSERT

Strawberry Delightful!

8ounces cream cheese

12 ounces of strawberry pie filling

1 can of condensed milk

¼ cup lemon juice

1teaspoon of vanilla extract

1 pound cake (store bought)

1 pint of fresh strawberries

1 can of whipcream

Directions:

In large mixing bowl, blend chesse and milk for 5 minute. Then add lemon juice, and vanilla in the mixer.

In a large wine glass, layer strawberries, pie filling, cream chesse, whipcream and pound cake. Top with whipcream and fresh strawberries. Chill 20 minutes and serve.

Apple Cobbler

1 can apple pie filling plus 4 peeled and slice green apple

1 ½ teaspoon lemon juice

2 tablespoons cinnamon

(2) 9" ready pie crust unbaked

½ cup butter melted

2 cups brown sugar

1/8 granulated sugar

½ cup milk

3 tablespoon corn starch

Directions:

In bowl, combine apple filling, apple, lemon juice, cinnamon, butter, and sugar, set aside.

In small mixing cup, combine milk and corn starch until dissolved. Pour over apple mixer.

In large casserole dish, place one pie crust on bottom, preheat oven 350oF place casserole dish in oven for 12 minutes until one pie crust is golden brown.

Then remove casserole dish from over, pour apple mixer onto brown crust add top crust. Prick the crust with a fork so no air bubbles will form.

Bake for 55 minutes 350o F, sprinkle granulated sugar lightly on top for flaky crust.

Peach Cobbler

1 can peach plus 4 fresh peaches washed, peeled, and slice

(2) 9 inch ready pie crust

2 cups brown sugar

½ stick butter

1/8 teaspoon salt

1/3 cup corn starch

½ cup milk

1 ½ teaspoon ground cinnamon

1 ½ teaspoon nutmeg

1 ½ teaspoon vanilla extract

1/8 granulated sugar

Directions:

In a casserole dish place one of pie crust in the bottom of dish. Place in oven at 350oF for 12 minutes until brown, set a side.

In mix bowl, combine peach, sugar, butter, salt, cinnamon, nutmeg, and vanilla, stir well, set a side

In small mixing cup, add milk and corn starch stir until dissolved. Pour over peach mixture.

Add remain crust on top bake for 55 minutes. Brush butter on top of pie crust, sprinkle granulated sugar on top for flaky crust.

Sweet Potato Casserole

3 cups cooked, mashed sweet potatoes

½ cup brown sugar

½ cup melted butter

½ tsp salt

1 teaspoon vanilla extract

¼ cup milk

Topping: Pecan Mix

½ cup brown sugar

¼ cup corn starch

2 Tbsp butter softened

¾ cup Pecans chopped

Directions:

Combine sweet potatoes ,sugar, butter, salt, vanilla, egg and milk, blend well for 5 minutes, set aside.

In separate bowl, combine brown sugar and flour stir in half pecans.

Combine and mixpotatoes and other half of the pecan. Spread in a greased 2 quart baking dish. Top with the remaining pecans and bake at 350oF for 15 minutes.

Bread Pudding

¼ cup unbleached flour

½ cup brown sugar

½ teaspoon cinnamon

1/8 teaspoon salt

¼ teaspoon nutmeg

1 teaspoon vanilla extract

3 eggs beaten

3 tsblespoons butter melted

3 cups milk (scalded-almost to a boiling point)

1 ½ cup dry bread cubes

½ cup raisins or dates if desired

Combine in 1 ½ or quart casserole flour, sugar, cinnamon, salt, nutmeg ,vanilla, egg, butter, and scalded milk. Blend well and stir in bread cubes and raisins.

Bake at 350oF for 45 -60 minutes. Stick knife into bread pudding, if knife comes out clean pudding is done. Top with lemon sauce.

Lemon Sauce

¼ cup butter softened

1 cup confectioner sugar

1 egg york (only yellow part of the egg)well beaten

1 tablespoons hot water

2 teaspoons lemon juice

1 teaspoon grated lemon rind

Put butter and sugar in top of double boiler. Add egg and hot water in top double boiler. Place over boiling water in botton down boiler. Beat until smooth and glossy. Remove from heat add lemon juice and lemon rind. Serve over bread pudding warm.

Dedication Page

I designed this cookbook to help anyone wanting to cook smart not hard especially for those that want to stop spending so much money eating out rather eating at home and enjoying family time at the dinner table. Your kitchen should be the heart of your home. This book allows you to enjoy preparing the foods you like easily, quickly and being proud of your finished meal.

While growing up I loved to watch my mother cook. I stay around her watching her every move. When the time came for me to learn how to cook, she allowed me to stir, chop, peel and yes mix. Every so often, she would let me cook small meals like toast. While cooking with my mother I dreamed that one day I could cook for people and watch them enjoy eating it.

Several years ago, I assisted my sister in her barbecue business by cooking side dishes such as sweet potato pies, fresh greens, hot water cornbread just to name a few. I started reflecting on the time I spent with my mother in the kitchen. I enjoyed watching people eat the good food I prepared. Later on, I stated working part-time at a local grocery store in the meat department. This opportunity allowed me to open my eyes and dream once more that God had a plan for my life, a cook book!

I wrote this book in loving memory of my mother Thressie Lee Oliver who was a wonderful mother, friend, and cook. I believe that is was her destiny to write a cookbook but God placed the vision in me to remember all the great recipes she created for her family. God has a plan for you, yield to the Holy Word and the voice of God for your life. My name is Dorothy Oliver Massey, enjoy this cookbook! Holiday book coming soon.

Acknowledgment page

I like to thank my parents Otha Oliver Sr. and Thressie Lee Oliver for creating and love all of their children. Thanks to my children Antwaine and Monique for being great children and giving me two beautiful grandchildren Ty and Arial. A special thanks to all my siblings, nieces, nephews and friends. Also, special thanks to my spiritual leaders Pastor Johnson Beaven III & Citadel of Faith COGIC, and Pastor Jerome & Laby Genise Barber & Harvest Rain Ministries Church. Remember God has a plan for your life; it was predestinated before the beginning of the world. Yield to the word and voice of God and he will give you clear directions and instructions for your life. Are you in his will?

Biography page

I was born in Indianapolis, Indiana, to Otha Oliver Sr. and Thressie L Oliver. I'm the fifth of seven children and the mother of two children and two grandchildren. My hobbies are cooking, gardening, and now writing. I'm also a member of Concern Clergy of Indianapolis and prayer leader of Citadel of Faith COGIC.

Equivalent measures and weights

Pinch or dash less than 1/8 teaspoon

3 teaspoons 1 Tablespoon

1 ½ teaspoons ½ Tablespoon

4 tablespoons ¼ cup

5 tablespoons 1/3 cup

8 tablespoons ½ cup

12 tablespoons ¾ cup

16 tablespoons 1 cup

2 cups 1 pint

4 cups(2 pint) 1 quart

4 quarts (liquid) 1 gallon

8 quarts (dry) 1 peck

4 pecks (dry) 1 bushel

2 tablespoons 1 fluid ounce

1 cup 8 fluid ounces

1 quarts 32 fluid ounces

Printed in the United States
by Baker & Taylor Publisher Services